Strawb
Milkshake

Risham
Zakaria

Honestly, there is nothing to talk about me. I write for fun. But if there is one thing that can describe me, I am funny. No. Of course, I am not. I am the most boring guy you will ever know. Beat it. Anyway, thanks for purchasing.

Risham Zakaria
Kuala Lumpur,
Malaysia

One can escape from people, places, and miseries, but one can never escape from death.

Table of Contents

Strawberry Milkshake

How could you behave like that? Everything ruined. I don't know why I listened to you. I look like a fool in there. How am I going to face them tomorrow? *I'm...* Don't, don't say any more words.

Silent engulfed.

A few people scattered about in the restaurant, where Roberto was sitting against the couch near the dusted glass panel. Sunlight penetrated through it, showering Roberto's face. But, the morning sunlight wasn't hot. A couple was sitting at the back, beside the backdoor. Their giggles made it through the area, reverberating. Roberto stared at them. They seemed unbothered, continuing their giggles. At the middle table, a bespectacled man with a checkered shirt was reading a newspaper, in his world or another part of the world, depending on his reading. Roberto was fascinated by how he could bear those noises. The place was a usual hangout spot for teenagers. After lunch hour, students from neighboring schools thronged this place. But today, there were none of them. Located in the outskirt town, the restaurant was decorated with a retro diner theme. A bit odd but it was unique. A hit song from the '80s was played in the background, recreating an old American vibe. The foods, though, were mid. But its milkshake was the best in town, if not the country. Roberto looked around, waiting for someone to serve him.

"Excuse me," he said, waving his hand.

The waitress, in her early twenties, running back and forth between the kitchen and the cash counter, seemed chaotic and unorganized. Her decayed-looking eyes could be mistaken for a brain lust character from a Hollywood movie Roberto watched last weekend. She took orders from the couple and returned to the counter, running back and forth between places. Exhausting even for Roberto. She brought a meal to the man in the middle seat. Roberto waved his hand again, attempting eye contact. He tried to make it obvious. The couple looked at him and whispered among themselves. His legs trembled. His palms began to wet.

Did you see that? Nobody gives a damn about us. He paused for a few seconds, and he continued. This is all your fault. You are stupid. Ever since you were a kid, nobody liked you. Your mom hated you. Your dad left you. You have no friends. Do you remember the day you cried when nobody picked you to be on their soccer team? Nobody wants to be your friend. *They picked me...* Yes, they picked you last because they had no choice, idiot. You are a burden to everyone. Even that girl ignored you. Roberto pointed his hand toward the waitress. Don't you realize it? Everyone here is laughing at you now. The couple is laughing at you. They must be pitying you, whispering about your past. About what you have done. I am ashamed. I shouldn't be here with you. *Let's fix this.* Shut up! Roberto's voice reverberated in the air.

"Excuse me, sir," an old woman said. She was sitting at the nearby table. Though she was there earlier, Roberto didn't realize her presence even with a vibrant-colored blouse that made her go unnoticed even from miles away. Such lousy taste, Roberto thought to himself.

"Yes?" Roberto said.

"Whom are you talking to?" she asked.

Roberto stared at her, saying no word.

"Sorry," she said, slightly nodding her head.

Roberto grinned as he saw the old woman murmuring to herself. A few lines of wrinkles could be seen making their mark under her eyes. She tried to cover it with a foundation to no avail. The old woman was around his mother's age. Thinking about his mother, it had been a few months since they had lost contact. It was not that he didn't want to call her; it was just that he found nothing to talk about. His mom could be irritating sometime. To her, Roberto was still a kid. Not that Roberto hated her; it was just that she reminded him of everything that happened in the past. The past that Roberto tried hard to erase.

While sitting, he saw a few pedestrians walking on the pavement beside the road. There was a woman with a kid. A couple was strolling with their children. A middle-aged man was jogging. Some people were running errands. The cars were scarce. Only one or two were passing by.

Now everyone is going to think that I am crazy. Roberto said as he rested his arms on the table. This is all on you. We must end this when we get home. You must leave. Roberto lowered his voice. You will have to go, or I will make you go. *Please.* The waitress swooped beside Roberto before he realized it.

"I am so sorry. It is a bit hectic in here today. Can I have your order? We have everything on the menu," she said, wiping sweat on her left cheek.

Roberto, startled at first, stared at her for a few seconds and said, "I need a menu."

"Oh, sorry. I'll get one for you." She said. She looked over her shoulder, and when she was about to turn her body, Roberto stopped her.

"Never mind. Can I have a set of fish and chips? And a strawberry milkshake," Roberto said.

"All right, sir," she said.

I am lactose intolerant. Shut your mouth.

"Pardon me?" she said. Her face was crinkled.

"That's all," Roberto said.

The waitress headed towards the kitchen, sticking the note on the kitchen wall. Then, she brought the orders to the couple, who seemed to stop giggling. The man thanked the waitress. Roberto observed them from his sitting.

I am sorry. I didn't mean to do it. I had no idea. Roberto folded a tissue in front of him. *I got triggered when he talked to me like that. I don't know why I became like that. I regret that it turned out that way.* Roberto said no word.

We are going to talk about this at home. I am not going to let people think I am crazy. I had had enough of people talking behind my back. You see the old woman beside us. She has been peeking at us since we got here. She must be thinking that I had lost my mind. You know I am not mad at you. I am mad at myself. I am the one to be blamed. I make you look weak. I make you become a pushover. Everybody steps all over you. They don't respect you. *No, it's my fault.* Roberto paused when he saw the waitress heading toward him, bringing his orders. She put a plate of fish and chips and a glass of strawberry milkshake.

"Enjoy your meal," she said.

"Where is my order?" the old woman said in a raised voice. Roberto looked at her. The woman seemed annoyed that her order was nowhere to be seen even though she had come earlier than Roberto. Roberto grinned. Serve you right, Roberto thought to himself.

The waitress apologized to the woman. She dashed to the kitchen as if she was flying.

Could you order me a coke? Roberto didn't reply. *I am thirsty. Please.* Roberto cut the fish into pieces with a knife. He dipped one of the pieces using a fork with mayonnaise and put it into his mouth. He swallowed the fish slowly. Then, he gulped the strawberry milkshake. He nodded as he savored the meal. Roberto seemed satisfied.

The waitress came again with the old woman's order in her hands. The woman breathed out and thanked the waitress as she was saying sorry again. The woman was about to say something, but she halted. As the waitress was making her way, Roberto called her.

"Hey,"

"Yes, sir," she said.

"Do you have coke?"

She nodded.

"One large size, please,"

She nodded again, affirming the order.

Thank you. Roberto continued enjoying the plate. He swallowed every piece of fish and chips into his mouth. He gushed them with the milkshake. It had been a month since he last had his favorite meal.

I want to become a writer. I want to write. Roberto chewed what was inside his mouth. *I want to tell my story.* Roberto swallowed the milkshake, rinsing his throat. He put the fork and knife on the plate as he released a belch. There were pieces of fish left, and a bit of chip remained untouched. What did you say? You want to write. Roberto chuckled. He seemed amused. I spent much time making a living. I worked hard to pay the bills. I studied for many years to get a job that pays well. Just when I thought to settle down, you ruined everything. And now you are talking about your bloody hobby. *It's not a hobby.* Then what is it? *It's my passion.* Roberto didn't say anything. He raised his eyebrows. Passion? Can it pay the bills? Can it put the meals on the table? I was the one who paid for your typewriter. You don't even have money. You can't write. Nobody wants to publish your rubbish. Nobody wants to read your stuff. Forget it. Roberto picked up the fork but put it back afterward. You ruin my appetite. *I'm sorry.* Do not say sorry. Just don't. I hate it. Roberto clenched his teeth.

The old woman stood up, heading towards the counter. There was still a big portion left on her plate. She glanced over her shoulder, looking at Roberto. She shook her head as she whispered something to the waitress at the counter. After a moment, she left the restaurant through the main glass door. She took one final look at Roberto before crossing the road to the other side. Roberto didn't notice. His mind was somewhere else.

A moment later, a man who was like the Empire State building walked into the restaurant. His stature alone caught everyone's attention. He wore a red cap with a black football shirt and a pair of blue jeans. The alpha look he had made him attractive to both genders. As he walked past the counter, he smiled at the waitress.

"Welcome, sir," she said with a wide smile.

He headed towards the corner table. The waitress pursued him. He made himself comfortable on the couch. Even when he sat, his head was protruding in the air. Roberto didn't realize his presence at first, but when he did, his hand started to tremble. Roberto stood up and walked to the counter. He could feel his legs start shaking. His palms grew wet. He stood at the counter waiting for the waitress to attend to him. She came a moment later.

"20 dollars," she said as she skimmed through the bill.

"Where's my coke? Please hurry." Roberto said. She seemed confused at first but realized it after a moment.

"Oh, sorry, sir. I forgot to tell you that our soft drink machine is out of order," she said.

Roberto handed her 20 dollars and two pieces of 10 dollars notes.

"Thank you, sir. See you around," she said.

Roberto stepped out. Looking over his shoulder, he could see the man was staring at him. Now the man's face was more apparent. He waved at Roberto. Roberto didn't respond. He walked out, avoiding eye contact. Silent pursued as Roberto walked through the pavement. He peeked at his watch. It was almost 3 PM. The warm wind blew over his face. Most of the people were indoors. Only a few were walking on the pavement. Some were in the restaurant, some in the bookstore, and some in the grocery store. *I am thirsty. Can you stop at that convenience store for a moment?* Roberto hesitated but walked to the store after a short pause. The convenience store was located at the corner lot beside the junction. Roberto had to walk a few meters to get there. It may not be far, but the weather had triggered the sweat glands to release the salty liquid.

“Welcome,” a young boy said as Roberto entered the store. He looked fresh, maybe a school leaver, Roberto thought.

“Red Marlboro,” Roberto said.

The boy picked a pack of Marlboro from the rack behind him and handed it to Roberto. Roberto gave him the money. *Could you buy me a coke?* Roberto walked out. Once outside, Roberto ruffled his pocket and picked a lighter. He lit a cigarette in his mouth. He coughed a bit as he inhaled the smoke. *Please, stop it.* Roberto smoked without minding his surroundings. The smell of tobacco uplifted his energy. He took a deep breath after he exhaled the smoke. He coughed again.

On the other side of the road, Roberto saw a doughnut stall beside the sidewalk. Few people were lining up there. Roberto looked left and right. The zebra cross was far from where Roberto was standing. Roberto crossed the road as he saw no vehicle in his sight. *Don't.*

One red sedan was dashing towards him as Roberto reached the middle of the road. He saw the driver, a woman, when he was about to be hit. It was already late, he thought to himself. Is this the end of his life? He thought. The car crashed into him. Roberto soared. A loud bang echoed, penetrating the area. Roberto felt on the road. Time seemed to stall. The light faded. His limbs got colder. His heart beat hard. He could feel liquid start running down his head. Finally, he was about to die, Roberto thought. He closed his eyes. Flashes of memories came to him. The memories that he kept locked somewhere inside his brain. Everything played to him in one long movie. Roberto just let it come to him. He embraced every one of them.

People had already flocked to the area to attend to the fallen Roberto. He couldn't see any of them. No bleeding, one of the men shouted. Call the ambulance, someone murmured. Roberto tried to regain his thought, but everything was confusing. His mind was getting heavy. He was lying on the asphalt road under the blue sky with bruises all over his body. The thin layer of clouds couldn't halt the sunbeam. The driver sat in her wrecked car, dazing. Her eyes remained wide open.

An ambulance arrived with a loud siren a few moments later. The men in the crowd helped the EMT to put the unconscious Roberto on the stretcher. One EMT checked his pulse and pupil while pushing the stretcher into the ambulance.

Just after the EMT pulled the rear door, Roberto came back to his sense. He exhaled a heavy breath. The air came in and out through his lung. He pushed the hand of the other EMT as he tried to put the ventilator tube into his mouth.

"Where am I?" Roberto said.

"You are in the ambulance, sir. You just had an accident. Could you tell me your name, sir?" one of the EMTs said.

Roberto seemed bewildered. He rubbed his temple.

"I am thirsty. Can you get me a coke?" he said.

The EMTs stared at each other bemused.

Goodbye

I have had trouble sleeping for days. Even if I try to shrug it off, my mind keeps coming back to it. I will be up in the blue sky in a few minutes. Thinking about it, my hand trembles, and my heart explodes. A hint of sweat is making its way all over my flesh, running down from my temple to my chin. My brain is making a cocktail of feelings. What if the plane breaks up mid-air? What if the engine fails? What if the pilot commits suicide? I had seen it happens in movies, though.

My father insisted I join. Our first official family trio, he murmured every time he had a chance. I argued that this would be our second. He seemed to have forgotten that when I was little, he brought me to Singapore. 'That doesn't count,' he smirked.

Ladies and gentlemen, this is the final boarding call for flight ML730 to Jakarta. Please proceed to gate 3 immediately.

I run like a headless chicken. Can a headless chicken run? That is not for me to figure out. My eyes lurk around, looking for 'Gate 3'. A woman on the east side of the airport waves at me. Thank god. I hand her my passport and the boarding pass. I would be drenched in sweat if not for the air-conditioning. She smiles and allows me to board the plane. She later attends to some rough passengers arguing with her male colleague. I stroll on the sky bridge that leads to inside the fuselage. A 6-foot tall stewardess shows my seating which locates on the aisle. I put my belongings in the upper compartment. The two passengers who argued earlier enter the cabin, heading towards their respective seats. Another stewardess starts counting and checking the manifest. As the light dims over time, the captain announces the take-off and asks the crew to be ready.

A roar of the engines reverberates as the plane dashes on the runway. I close my eyes, praying. Little by little, I can feel gravity pull my weight down. I hold my breath. The clock hits 12 when the flight soars in the sky. I am now thousands of feet above in the sky. Occasional shakes occur whenever the wings cut through thick clouds. The city glimmered in the light scattering on the ground. The moon in the sky makes the view looks majestic.

Sa-yo-na-ra, Kuala Lumpur.

Amen

Death and despair test a man in his darkest hours. And I found it to be true. When I lost someone I loved, I was ready to die. I figured life had no meaning after all. We worked hard to achieve our dream, just to be shattered by death.

Is life worth fighting for? Does life have any meaning? I started thinking about everything. Life, death, relationship, happiness. All intertwine in my mind. Why are we looking for it, if at the end, we are going to lose it? Nobody will remember us when we die except the people who love us. But they aren't going to live forever. They will die too. At some point, no single soul will remember us. We are just specks of dust in this gigantic universe.

For that reason, nothing matters.

Grit

Sun shines; air blows. I stroll along the pavement through the throng. My head is spinning with cocktails of feelings. My heart pumps blood in and out. I keep walking towards nowhere. *"Move away."* Somebody whisper. Sweat rushes out of my skin. I grip the strap, the dog guides me aside. Huge relief.

Big Bad Wolf

Once upon a time, animals and humans lived in harmony in a faraway land for many centuries. They breathed the same air; they obeyed the same rules – they wouldn't kill each other either for devour or lust. Even at first, many among the animals were reluctant to follow the rules, but they later succumbed. Once famously known as murderous beasts, wolves were among the last signatories to the treaty. If not for the tiger, the pack wouldn't stamp their emblem to the indenture many hoped would last generations. And the peace remained the way their ancestors were hoping until one occurrence that, to date, remained debatable in the scholastic circle.

Big Bad Wolf was the name he was identified (as per the treaty, an animal should be referred to based on their gender). His birth name was widely disputed by modern historians. However, based on the Annals of the Malay Archipelago, the only surviving record referred by researchers, he was known as Serigala. Serigala was the 10th generation after the treaty was put into place. His father was slaughtered by a hunter when he was still a pup. Since then, he had been surviving alone. He never met his mother. He never knew he had one until he reached his teenage ages. But he never tried to look for her. Serigala also had no idea how his father died, but everybody said he was murdered by some people. So, he looked forward to avenging him one day. But he was cowardly. His body was frail. And humans were the last things he wanted to encounter.

His father, a gentle wolf, was a respectable wolf among the animals and human community. As a professor of history at a nearby university, every wolf in the pack looked at him with adoration. No wolf had ever achieved that accomplishment before. His death had shaken the community a bit. Many still carried the pain.

Since his father's demise, Serigala had avoided humans. Loneliness had bit by bit, taken control of his mind. Sometimes, he thought he was someone else. Things became worse when one night, he woke up in the middle of the night drenched in sweat, his leg trembled, and his heart raced. Two men were chasing him; one was holding a chainsaw, and the other with an ax. But he didn't run away. He embraced them. He waited for them to get closer so that he could pounce on them. The urge to prey on them and devour their meat conquered his brain. He thirsted for their blood. He took a deep breath in and out and closed his eyes, but the nightmare was still in motion. Was it a nightmare? He thought. He got up and went to his study, reading the annals until the sun knocked on the surrounding with its sunbeam.

In the morning, Serigala prepared his breakfast; mushroom soup and wild berries. While breakfasting, he saw a girl with a red scarf heading toward his house. The blood rushed all over his body. His heart pumped in and out. He clenched his teeth. Serigala was sitting on the bench in front of his house when the girl stopped by the front gate.

"Excuse me, sir," the girl said loudly.

Serigala pretended not to hear it. He kept swallowing the wild berries on the plate that depleted over time. When the wild berries were gone, he gulped the hot soup directly from the bowl that later burnt his tongue and lips. The bowl fell onto his lap, making the pain became worse. He gasped for air to lessen the misery.

"Are you okay, sir?" the girl said as she dashed towards him. She offered him the bottle she was carrying in the basket.

"I got some red wine," she said.

Serigala took the bottle without hesitation. The pain seemed to surpass his spinelessness. He guzzled the wine until the last drop. Some spilled over his shirt. It was the first time he had ever tasted wine.

"I am sorry," Serigala said as he returned the empty bottle.

"It's okay, sir. My granny hates red wine anyway. She prefers the white one, but we run out of it," she said.

"Your grandmother?"

"Yes. I was about to ask you just now. I am on my way to her house. My mom said it is located in the south of the river. But the road seems different. I think I am lost. Maybe I had taken a wrong turn. Thank god I see your house," She said in delight.

Serigala felt dizzy. His head became heavy like someone put stones over it. He tried to apprehend what she was saying, but his mind was blurry. The wine seemed to be invading his body, engulfing his blood and taking control of his mind. The red wine that looked like blood had triggered something in him. Never had blood in his life. The temptation alone had boosted his dopamine. But he was still spineless. What if someone saw him? He would be hanged or roasted. His remains would be fed to pigs. He would be sealed as a monster in a history book. He tried to fight the urge. But her scent was too hard to bear. Just one time, he promised himself. He gathered his thought. The girl was expecting his reply.

"Sorry. A bit dizzy. Could you please say it one more time? And your name?"

"I am Little Red-Scarf. May I know which road I should take if I want to go to the south of the river?" she said, a slight smile curved on her mouth.

"Oh dear, you are not lost. You are on the right path. But it would take some time to reach your destination. You have to be quick before the sun sets. Along the way, you would find a sunflowers field, a garden full of colorful tulips and roses, and bushes with thousands of wild berries and nuts. You could take some for yourself. Just be aware of the walking trees and river of blood."

"River of blood?"

"Oh, sorry. I meant,... *flood*."

"Oh, I see. Thank you so much, Mr...err...what should I call you?" Little Red-Scarf said.

"Mr. Wooff, you call me Wooff," he said.

"Thank you, Wooff. I don't know how I can repay your kindness. I hope our paths shall cross again sometime. I have to hurry before the sun goes down."

"Sure. No problem. *See you soon*."

The girl went on a walk with a spring in her steps. She took the left turn looking over her shoulder and waved at Serigala. He smiled and waved back awkwardly.

As the girl was nowhere to be seen in his sight, Serigala stood up and decided to pursue the girl. The girl picked some mulberries along the path, humming and giggling. The girl decided to stop at a giant oak tree. She then plucked the white flowers underneath the trees and put them in the basket. She continued walking until she reached the junction. There were two ways; one on the left led to the grandmother's house, while the right would take some time which had been told by Serigala to possess all the flowers and berries in the area. She turned right. Serigala smirked. A small victory for him. he thought.

He dashed towards the grandmother's house via the left road. He galloped using all his hands and legs (as per the treaty, animals should not walk or run using their hands, and the hands should never be called legs) until his armpits and crotch were flooded with sweat.

When he arrived, he saw a house standing near the river. He guessed that it must be the grandmother's house. He trotted, heading to the back of the compound. He looked around over his shoulder to see anyone around, but he saw no one, neither human nor animal, in the vicinity. He stepped towards the house and peeked through the window. A frail old lady was lying on the bed. A loud snoring could be heard. She was sick, he presumed. He knocked at the back door.

"Who's there?" the old woman said.

"I am your grandchild, Little Red-Scarf," Serigala replied softly, trying to imitate the little girl.

"What are you doing at the back door? Come inside from the front. It's unbolted," she said.

Hearing that, Serigala thought everything was going according to his plan. Another victory, he murmured. He opened the front door, and before the old lady screamed her breath out after she saw him, the wolf jumped on her and gulped her whole body. He regretted it afterward, not because of his remorse, but because he had told himself earlier to devour the flesh instead of swallowing the whole body. And the old lady tasted weird. He still had the girl, he assured himself. He closed the door and rested his body on the bed after he wrapped his body in the old woman's blouse. He almost fell asleep under the bedclothes when he heard knocking on the front door.

"Who's there?" Serigala failed to imitate the woman's voice, but he was assured as his voice didn't sound like his own.

"I am Little Red-Scarf, your grandchild. My mom sent me to deliver cookies and berries. I also bring you some tulips and roses," the girl said.

"Come inside. The door is unbolted," he said, softening his voice.

The girl put the basket containing everything she carried on the table beside the bed. She saw her grandmother (a counterfeit grandmother, to be precise) lying on the bed. Looking at her like that, the girl felt pity towards her grandmother. She must have thirsted for the wine after so long in the bed. She took a glass of water from the kitchen and mashed some berries to put inside the water.

"How was your mother?" Serigala asked. He was still hiding under the bedclothes.

"She's doing great. She misses you, but she had to work."

"Come here and get into bed with me."

Little Red-Scarf brought the berries juice with her. She was amused when she figured her grandmother was wearing a blouse and said," Grandma, here is a glass of berries juice for you."

Serigala took a sip and gulped until the last drop. Even had wild berries every day in his entire life; he had never had this kind of drink before.

"It's delicious."

"I made it for you. I brought you a bottle of red wine. Even though red was not your taste, I thought it would somewhat boost your energy," the girl said.

"It's okay. The thing I just had was tastier than the wine. But what happened to the wine?"

"During my journey, I got lost. I was almost giving up. So, I walked along the way; I saw one adobe house enveloped by a wooden gate. I saw a man having his breakfast. I hesitated to interrupt him at first. I was desperate, so I asked him the route to come here anyway," she said and paused to check on her grandmother. And to her relief, her grandmother was still breathing.

"The man was handsome, but he was a bit shy, I believe. The soup he had burnt his mouth, so I gave him the wine to ease his pain. He seemed to like it so much, so I let him drink it. I felt relief when the hot soup didn't ruin his handsome face. He told me to bring you the flowers."

Serigala listened, and he found that the girl was thoughtful and nice. He was sober when he realized he shouldn't be in the house. It was a mistake, a huge one, he thought to himself. He murdered someone's grandmother. At that moment, he felt something moving in his stomach. It must be the old lady, he thought. She was still alive, to his shock.

"What big arms you have!" Little Red-Scarf said she opened the bedclothes.

"To hug you, my love."

"What big ears you have!"

"To listen to your voice, my love."

"What big eyes you have!"

"To see your beautiful face, my dear."

"What a big mouth you have!"

"To eat...err...to drink your delicious…juice, my child."

The counterfeit grandmother jumped out of bed, leaving the bedclothes on Little Red-Scarf, preventing her from witnessing the escape. She called out for her grandmother as she dashed to the front door. She saw her grandmother lying on the grass outside the house, drenched in liquid that the girl thought was sweat.

"Are you okay, grandmother?"

The old lady gasped a heavy breath as a corpse resurrected from the dead. She was bewildered, but she smiled after she saw her grandchild on her side. The girl led her grandmother in stepping inside. The old lady rested on her bed without saying anything. The girl got into the bed, hugging her grandmother. Her journey paid off, she told herself as she looked through the window at the blue sky.

Along the river, Serigala, who had been running from the house, stopped for a while to take some fresh air beside the river. He saw a woodcutter passing by on the path. The woodcutter saw him and smiled. He replied with a gesture. He had drained from all the running and the vomit. His head was wondering how he could swallow the whole body at ease, but it took all his muscles strained to spit out the old lady. He felt his life was reaching its peak; if it did, he just wanted to die a man, not a wolf. He slurped the water from the streaming river with his tongue. Under the blue sky, he promised never to touch the wine for the rest of his life.

The Last Feast

The sun had reclaimed its throne, radiating its energy to every quarter of the surrounding area. The thin layers of white clouds were floating in the air; their darker cousins had already gone somewhere. The downpour that had splashed the area for the past few days had washed all the dust and dirt, making trees and the grass greener and forcing human activities to halt. A hot bath was a blessing in this weather, and a cup of hot tea or coffee was extra. Lazy times for some people but miserable hours for many. In the southern parts of the town, houses sunk with the flood, damaging all belongings they had hoarded for years. Rivers and drains overflowed, converting roads to canals and vehicles to boats. While on this part of the town, located on the upper ground, people looked up to the sky while sipping hot tea and coffee.

The wind was biting my bone, freezing my mind to stone. Thank the sun, I could still sense my half-shivered limbs. The smell of the rain was lingering in the air as I was sitting in front of the compound. The playground was not here when I was little. All we had were sand and dirt, while on rainy days, we got mud that nearly got me murdered. My mom hated it. I hated it too. But the freshness of the air after the rain, I loved it. Frogs and crochets were working in the background, orchestrating their concerts. *Bravo!* the birds chirped afterward. I enjoyed this time of the day. I wished time had frozen at that moment. So I could stay in the moment forever. My wristwatch showed 5.00 PM. Only a few people were in the vicinity. A group of kids was hanging on the mowed grass beside the playground. The kids played with themselves, giggling and laughing without a slight worry. Some folks were walking and jogging, they seemed to be enjoying themselves.

"May I sit here young man?" an old remarked, motioning using his right hand towards an empty space on the damp bench. The old man was among the joggers. I didn't notice him earlier. His voice was familiar. I had heard this soothing voice somewhere.

I nodded as a sign of agreement. He took a deep and long breath after he made himself comfortable beside me. I glimpsed at him using the edge of my eyes, beads of sweat running down his face from his temple. The wrinkles below his slanted eyes were prevalent. The white had made their way to conquer the head. The black was counting its time before finally having to concede. The effect of telomere's shortening is taking place, I presumed. His eyes were fixed on the sky, deep.

"It's a good day, isn't it?" he said, breaking a pause. 'A good day' was an irony as the thunderstorm was the only show we had the entire morning. And it wasn't even a day yet. Many things happened and not everything was fine at least for me. I lost my job a few days ago and my body got sick. "Our policy has always been like this. We couldn't continue to hire you or, to be precise, people like you." The voice of the human resources manager was still spinning in my ears, lingering like flies. The dismissal was a blessing in disguise, I comforted myself. But for sure, it couldn't pay my outstanding bills. Maybe the old man and I have different ideas about a good day. The thoughts only remained in my head.

"Yes, it is a good day," I said, gazing at a black cat napping under the bench on the other side. It looked comfortable, undisturbed by the cold weather. Its fur was fluffy and groomed. Looking at his body, I presumed the was well-fed. Now I wish I were a cat. I could nap the whole day without having to worry about other things.

My brain was processing every bit of information in the archive to recall anything related to this not-so-familiar face. It was in the record, but like finding a book in a library, some books might go missing when you look for it. Some people who had thought to borrow the book changed their minds before checking out. They left it on a shelf nearby, not the right place. The same goes for idiots who thought it was appropriate to put a bottle of milk in the spices area, giving extra tasks to retail workers. The old man's voice reminded me of someone from the past, someone close to my father. Our faces might have evolved, but our voices remained the same for most people, including this old man.

"Usually, there were many kids at this time of the day. But this rain has stopped everything. This weather is comfortable, especially if you don't want to burn any calories and if you want to lay in your bed. Maybe having a cup of tea or coffee accompanied by banana fritters while enjoying the cold air," he said and paused for a moment. He gave a slight cough. Then he continued, "I prefer tea without sugar. When you are at this age, you will someday catch one or all of those diseases. You got to be very particular about everything you consume." He gazed at the compound, looking at the kids as they were cracking up, laughing over something. Seemingly over the jokes, one of the boys cracked. I could sense the emptiness in his gaze. He was looking at them, but his mind was somewhere out of this place, not in this playground or this town. Only his vessel stayed beside me.

I didn't say a word but nodded my head. This old man reminded me of my dad, who fancied decaffeinated and sugarless tea. My dad had diabetes, but his departure wasn't because of that; it was a heart attack that took his life. Myocarditis, the doctor said. No matter how often my mom told him to stop smoking, he never caved in. Unlike my dad, this old man talked to me.

"Is the playground newly built?" I said, regretting afterward. I lost control over my mouth. I wasn't the type to start a conversation, let alone to talk to an unfamiliar person. I either answer or listen. I prefer the latter. Even in class, teachers would bombard me with questions to make me say something. There was one time in a physics class when I pretended to be sick to avoid meeting the teacher, Mr. Ilyas. He seemed adamant about making me talk, which irritated me. Yet, I should thank him. If not because of him, I would not know who's Einstein or Edison.

"It was built around two months ago. Some rich guy donated us a huge sum of money. We didn't know what to do with it at first. Some suggested we build a badminton court, some suggested we repair the drains, and some said the drains were not our responsibility. Then, we decided to build this playground. We renovated the community hall with the money left." He paused and continued, "Have you been there?"

"No, I haven't. I just came back here a few days ago." I said.

"You should visit there. Its library has been stocked up with many books. A lot of English novels. You are surely going to love it." He said while gazing at his smartwatch. I was an avid reader. I loved books. As a kid, I asked my mom for extra pennies to buy a book which she reluctantly gave me. I didn't usually read it. I left it untouched for many weeks before taking a look. The smell of a new book was addictive. Before I came back to this town, I had to sell my collection of books, hundreds if not thousands of them. I hate the fact that it was the only choice.

"I'll go visit someday. Does it have Haruki Murakami's?" I said.

He stared at me with a bewildered face. "I don't know. I am not a reader. But they have plenty of new novels."

"I see"

"How's your mom doing?" Now his soothing voice sounded fragile.

"She is doing great," I lied. I didn't talk to her, and she avoided me ever since I returned. She looked like the last time I had seen her six years ago. The hair was still silky and black. We lost contact after I left home. Even when my father passed away, I didn't come back to visit. Nobody told me about his passing. I believed it wouldn't make any difference even if I knew. Maybe this was the reason my mom avoided me. Did she hate me? This old man knew my mother; I presumed he knew everything.

"Your mom is a good cook. Your dad used to give me some."

My brain was suddenly electrocuted with new information. It had to be it, I said to myself.

My mom cooked chicken rice every Friday, which my dad would take to his workplace. He loved the chicken rice. This may be the only thing we had something in common. He worked as a welder in a steel factory in the nearby city. His friend, Mr. Adam, fetched him with a shabby Honda bike every weekday sharp at 7 AM. There was one time he came to our house. He waited for my father. My mother asked me to greet him. I walked to him, and when he touched my shoulder, I bit his index finger. I didn't know why I did that, but I did it anyway.

The urge to disappear rose inside me. My heart's beat pumped like there was no tomorrow. The blood raced in my veins, my face turned red. Luckily, my skin was dark enough to cover that. Sweat grew on my palms. I had been trying to avoid this old man since that day.

Mr. Adam stared at me. I hoped his old age had erased that part of memories out of his system. “How is your wife?” I asked, attempting to avoid the awkwardness. “She’s fine. She was at Ali’s house. His wife delivered a boy only a few weeks ago. Do you remember him?“ Mr adam said.

Ali was my friend, my childhood friend, to be exact. We became friends when I was a little boy. The first we met, well, it was not exactly fun. He and his twin took my truck toy and giggled on their way home. I cried for the whole day. It was my first defeat. After Imran died, my friendship with Ali faded away.

“How’s Ali doing, Mr. Adam,”

“He had been occupied with his newborn son. Everything is in a mess.”

“Is this his first child?” My curiosity went into first gear.

“This is his third child. He already had two daughters. When he got married, we decided to have a small ceremony. I was at first reluctant to let them -- he and his girlfriend -- get married. I'm not sure whether you know his wife. Her name is Sarah." He said.

"I don't know her. Maybe I will if I look at her face,"

"Youth at your age are headstrong, millennials' trait. They call it love. But for me, it is immature. How do you want to support your family with no regular job or fixed income? Is love enough to pay the bills and put meals on the table? Marriage is not about making love and having fun. It is commitment and responsibility. But after all, what could I do? I conceded after all the pleas. My wife agreed. She didn't want to prolong the issue." Mr. Adam wiped the sweat from his forehead and temple with his palm.

"My granddaughters love the swing," he said. His eyes were fixed on the playground.

"When did they get married?" I asked.

"Six years ago, if I recall correctly. When he was 17 years old. She was two years younger." He paused before he continued. "They got into big trouble weeks before the school graduation. It was a headache. The girl, my now daughter-in-law, didn't want to undergo an abortion. She pled with her father not to report Ali. My wife, too, talked with Sarah's parents. Ali and Sarah were in love. I should have paid more attention. I don't mind him getting arrested, as he should take responsibility. He deserved it."

"At least they are happy now, right?"

"His mom was the happiest grandmother in this town." He remarked with a trace of a smile on his face. The golden sunlight sparkled on his face. I breathed in and out. I felt my lung expand as the cold air sucked in. We sat there, silent. The kids were already gone. Now, we were the only humans in the area.

"When I was a kid, we didn't have gadgets. So we played outside a lot. My mom used to scold me when she found out I showered in the rain. At that time, I didn't think much about anything. I want to play. Schooltime was playtime. When I got home, I went to my friend's house to play. I didn't grasp how time worked back then. I thought I was going to stay a child forever. I thought my mom would always be there to protect me. But, in a blink, I grow old. My mom passed away when I was forty. Wrinkles were forming all over my face without me even realizing how they got there. Like salt in a container, we're delusional. It looks full one day, and in a few days, it's almost empty. But unlike time, we can always buy a pack of salt at the grocery."

He glanced at his smartwatch. "It's almost six," he said.

"Do you have any regret in your life, Mr. Adam?"

He didn't reply. Maybe he didn't hear what I said. Maybe he pretended not to hear. He seemed to ignore me for a moment. His gaze was on the sky while he stroked his furrowed brow. A couple of joggers walked past us. Mr. Adam didn't look at them. I bowed my head when they looked at me. They smiled in return.

"Of course, but I believe everything happens because we will only find it later. So I don't dwell on the past. Life goes on," he said. And he continued, "You shouldn't waste your energy on something you cannot do anything about. Appreciate what you have in your life, and don't take things for granted."

He got up and stretched his body left and right. "I got to go now. It was nice talking to you, Faris. You resemble your father," he reached out his right hand. "Before I forget, tonight, we will have a small thanksgiving feast for my grandson. Ali won't be there, but I hope you can come," he continued while gripping my hand. I nodded. "God's willing," I said.

He walked at a slow pace towards the residential blocks on the east. My eyes were fixed on his stature. Before I realized it, he was out of my sight. The sun was heading west, preparing to serve on the other part of the sphere. A flock of birds surfed in the skies, making their way to their nest in the east. The cat had disappeared. The sensor in the lampposts had been triggered. The day was ready to depart. I stood up and forced my move home even though my legs were unready.

My house was located only a few corners from the playground. I strolled, taking my time to appreciate the dimming surrounding area. The road was still wet and puddled. There was a large and deep pothole in the middle of it. I sneezed as the cold wind blew over my face. I hate cold weather. As I took the first corner, I realized a black cat with a yellow collar around its neck was pursuing me. I wasn't sure whether it was the cat I had seen earlier. Maybe it was, but it looked slimmer when I looked closer. When I stopped walking, it also stopped crawling. I used a verbal cue to attract it, but it didn't respond. It stood with caution, maintaining the posture and the distance. It stared at me for a moment. As I stepped closer, the cat dashed out of my sight. I restarted my trip back home.

My mom was already at home when I got there. She had been out since the afternoon. I opened the main door and saw her already dressed in a plain pink blouse with a black scarf. "What's the occasion?" I said. She ignored me. She grabbed the keys hanging on the wall. "Dinner's on the table." She said and closed the door behind her. That was the first time I heard her voice after years. I sat on the couch, resting my body as I had just crossed the finish line in a marathon.

The smell of coffee wafted through the air. I stood up and walked to the kitchen. I took a cup of coffee and decided to bathe first before dinner. The warm water from the heater saved me from getting frozen. Half an hour was enough to get me clean. My body felt new, like a newborn; it felt fresh. But it couldn't erase what Mr. Adam had said. Everything he said lingered in my head. And it reminded me of my predicament.

My entire world went into shambles the day I got the news. I, for the first time in my life, prayed to god to turn back the clock for me to avoid making some decision, some mistake.

Deep inside, I knew I couldn't promise that I would not make the same mistake even if god granted my wish. I cried and secluded myself for days, taking emergency leaves from work and ignoring calls from friends and colleagues. Suicidal thought was floating over my mind. If only I had found a painless way to execute, I would be talking from six feet under. It has to be a mistake, I told myself. Weeks later, I embraced reality and learned how to live with it.

"If you keep the routine properly, you could live normally. Make sure you take the pills on time," The doctor said. He sounded like he was reading from a script. He had done this many times, I assumed.

I wiped my body with a towel and got myself dressed. The dinner was already cold but still delicious. Mr. Adam was right. I swallowed the pills that the doctor gave me. I decided to hit the sack afterward. The pills had gotten my head swelling like it was being pumped. I distracted myself, counting from one to a thousand.

Before I reached two hundred, I found myself running in a wild swathed with darkness. Something big and monstrous was chasing to pound me. My heart was beating.

The fact that I could die at any moment taunted me. Not this way, I told myself. I wanted to die with my body remaining intact, not as a carcass. No. I wanted to live. There were many things that I wanted to achieve. I wanted to live longer. I wanted to cry; I wanted to scream for help. Even I knew no one would hear me. The wild was thick. The bushes were thick. The air was thick. The sky was dark and thick. I didn't know where I was heading but kept running. I ran to find a way out. Drips of sweat were flowing out of my skin. How long can I keep running? My legs were cramping. Should I let my body be scourged by the predator? I was part of the food chain, after all. I stopped running. I glanced over my shoulder, and I noticed the creature wasn’t in the vicinity. I lay on the forest bed and waited for the beast to capture me any moment, devouring every ounce of my meat. I heard the cracking of fallen wood. A moment later, a massive tiger lurked into the scene from behind the bushes. It was about to jump over me when I closed my eyes. As I opened it, I was not in the wild but in my house's kitchen. The sight was different, but my heart was still beating fast.

The darkness had enveloped the area. The only light source was my phone, which blinked, almost synchronizing with my heartbeat; family and friends were asking about my condition. "I am fine. Don't worry," I told them and promised to keep them updated. I was standing on the dining table while looking at the rising water. Hoping the rain would stop, I prayed to god. I calmed myself. Before I realized it, the water level had gone up. My heartbeat had gone up too. The cold water was biting my knees, numbing my limbs. I wrapped up my arms, keeping myself warm. I heard boat propulsion outside; what a relief. But the sound was getting further and further away until I heard nothing but gushing water. I panicked. They would turn back, I said to myself. Please come back. Please. They have yet to return. I heard frequent knocks on the back door.

My half-awake consciousness was still in the open house. "Faris, wake up. Mr. Adam had passed away." All at once, my consciousness arrived. It was my mom who knocked on the door at 7 AM. I looked at my mom and expected her to continue. "During morning prayer, in the mosque. He collapsed afterward." She said while making good of her scarf, the same black scarf she was wearing last night. I stayed silent while my mind tried to comprehend the situation. "Was he sick?" I said. "He had been sick for many years. He stopped getting chemo last month. He was fine last night. He even told me he met you yesterday. I should get going. Will you come?" She said and hurriedly walked out. I stared at the ceiling. Mr. Adam's voice was like a cloud passing by the blue sky.

You

I wish we had never met, but we did. When I saw you that day, my heart tickled. My palms grew wet. Is there any fragrance that could suck someone's soul? I would like to purchase it too.

"Is everything okay?" You said. Your voice, I almost mistook it for an angel's. Not that I knew how it sounded. If your voice were recorded, I would play it over and over until I get bored. No. I won't get bored.

When you looked at me, I looked somewhere else. *Please don't put me under your spell. Please.* I was miserable enough. If I were born a witch, I wish I could stop time. So we could have our moment. Even if the world perishes, the speck of time I got to be with you would be the one I cherish the most. Why God created you if not to be mine?

Final Destination

I am scared of death. The fact that we all are going to die someday shivers my bone. But today, I was ready to die. The feeling of readiness was different. *Come at me, full force.*

It wasn't the first time I got stuck inside a lift. Today, it was different. I was alone. I was shaken a bit at first, but I didn't panic. Maybe it was because my mind was focusing on something else. Toilet. I hate to admit it, but I was ready to let the liquid out inside the lift. I tried to remain calm to save every ounce of dignity if I managed to get out alive. The probability of someone getting man trapped is minimal. So, I questioned God why he chose me.

I sat on the floor, contemplating every decision I made in life. What if I got stuck here until there was no oxygen left for me to inhale? Suck. I hate to be in this situation.

Final Destination. Goddamn it. Why at this time?

It was February. I already hate my life again.

The end...